Good morning boys and girls, I'm about to get my day on

I'll head to school first to take a test I'll get an "A" on

Whoa! Before I go, here's a topic that I have a lot to say on

Here are a couple things I learned from a crayon

Boys and girls: this is what we call a play on words

Not a play on dogs, cats, or a play on birds

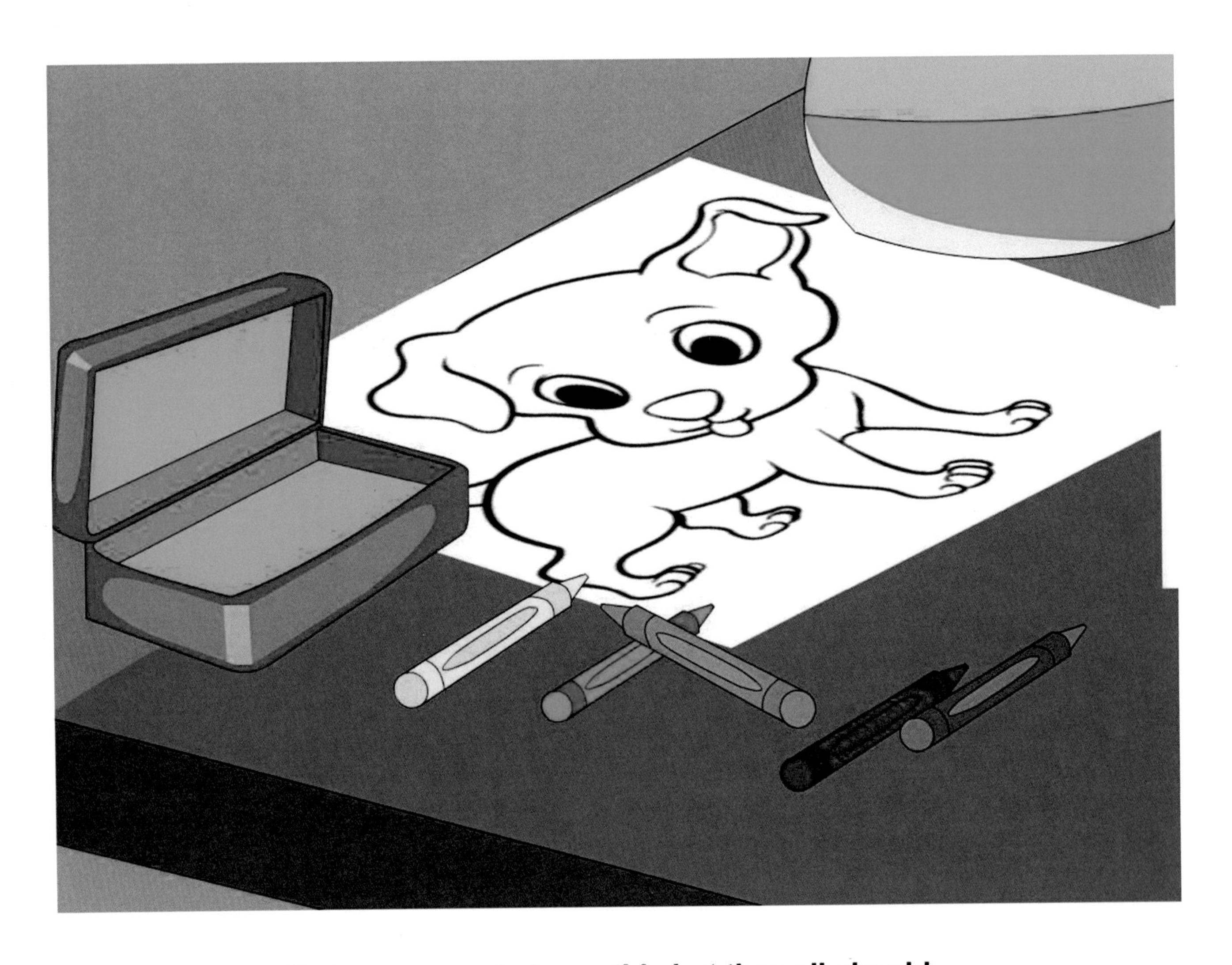

Not many people know this but they all should

I'm about to teach you something only a crayon could

Think about it, colors.. they can teach us about others

Like we don't need hate, all of us can be lovers

All of us can be sisters; all of us can be brothers

We should speak to others the same we speak to our mothers

Every day is a fight; we fight and argue a lot

Seems like no one does anything to make the arguing stop

I'll do whatever it takes to help for it to stop

Because I see crayons make it work with 24 to a box

Blue never makes a stink if it runs into pink

He'd listen to her problems and he'd care what she thinks

Same as pink would stay mellow if she ran into yellow

They wouldn't turn and walk away, they'd hug and say hello

Hello hello hello, same when purple met violet

Things didn't get violent they laughed and kept on smiling

When silver met brown she wasn't scared to bring him around

They were talking over dinner and hitting the town

Getting it now? No different when red met green

Best friends right away and never said things mean

Aren't you glad that orange helped gray to prosper?

And how gold acted proper instead of hating on copper

We don't get the picture, without love we're getting sicker

Every bad thing you say, you have to give a nickel to nickel

The answer is treat everyone the same, it's very simple

We all don't look and sound alike, some of us periwinkle

You need to get the same thing I'm getting from this

You could agree or disagree but I've been getting at this

Crayons make it work and it's perfect, they all getting the gist

Without red, yellow, and blue the rest would never exist

We need each other to grow, we need each other to live

We need each other for hope, we need each other to give

We need each other to love, we need each other for this

Without me and without you then us doesn't exist

People don't think there's problems, I'm proving there are

Everyone of us is born with a beautiful heart

We don't use it as humans we fight til the confusion will start

When crayons work together they create some beautiful art

I hope this bought you to life, taught you what's right

That's why I'm pushing for change and I'm supporting the fight

If we keep living in the dark then we'll get caught in the night

We can't show our true colors until we're bought into light

Made in the USA
Lexington, KY
04 September 2018